KW-421-012

SHANNONBRIDGE LIBRARY

0 9 AUG 2002

2 2 DEC 2002

Books are on loan
for 21 days.
Overdue books
charged at €1.00
per wk. / part wk.

8-12

MENTOR
BOOKS

This Edition first published 2001 by

MENTOR BOOKS
43 Furze Road,
Sandyford Industrial Estate,
Dublin 18.

Tel. + 353 1 295 2112/3   Fax. + 353 1 295 2114
e-mail: admin@mentorbooks.ie

ISBN: 1-84210-074-2

A catalogue record for this book is available from the
British Library

Copyright © 2001 Stephanie Dagg

The right of Stephanie Dagg to be identified as the
Author of the work has been asserted by her in
accordance with the Copyright Acts.

All rights reserved. No part of this publication may be
reproduced, stored in a retrieval system, or transmitted in
any form or by any means electronic, mechanical,
photocopying, recording, or otherwise, without prior
written permission of the publisher.

*All the characters in this book are fictitious.
Any resemblance to actual persons, living or dead,
is purely coincidental.*

Cover Illustration: Nicola Sedgwick
Typesetting, editing, design and layout by
MENTOR BOOKS

Printed in Ireland by ColourBooks

1 3 5 7 9 10 8 6 4 2

CONTENTS

The Author

Stephanie Dagg

Stephanie Dagg lives in Innishannon, County Cork.

She is married to Chris and is mother of two children, Benjamin and Caitlín, and has been writing stories ever since she was a child. Originally from Suffolk in England, she moved to Cork in 1992.

To Cyril and Edith Bouts

My wonderful grandparents

1
Third Time Lucky

'I don't know!' exclaimed Mum suddenly. 'I think I must be mad to bring you lot back to France after our last two holidays here.'

'Not at all, Mrs D!' Kevin reassured her. 'There's that saying, "third time lucky", isn't there. This is our third holiday together so it's bound to be nice and quiet and peaceful and restful and . . .'

'. . . and boring!' Tom finished for him, pulling a face.

'Boring sounds just fine to me!' smiled Mum. 'Ready for a stop, guys? Here are some services. I know I'm dying for a good strong café crème.'

'And I could murder an ice cold Orangina!' piped up Kevin.

'I could murder two,' Tom bettered him.

'Milk for me!' Four-year-old Anna didn't want to be left out.

'Fine,' said Mum, indicating and carefully pulling off the autoroute and into the service area. She was getting used to driving on the 'wrong' side of the road, but it was still pretty nerve-wracking.

They all climbed out of the car. First out was

ten-year-old Tom Donoghue, closely followed by his best friend, Kevin Murphy, who was ten too. Tom's sister, Anna, tumbled out next, showering crayons everywhere. She'd been busy colouring while they'd been driving down from the ferry. Mum — Tom and Anna's mum — was last out. She stretched gratefully, glad to be out of the car for a while. She scooped up the crayons, tossed them back on Anna's seat and they headed for the coffee bar and ordered the drinks.

'Anyone hungry?' asked Mum.

Silly question. Of course they were hungry! The boys and Anna claimed to be starving so Mum put in an order for croissants and jam for everyone.

'Goodness, where do you put it all?' laughed Mum minutes later. 'Especially after those huge cooked breakfasts on the ferry this morning!'

'It's the French air,' explained Kevin, in a muffled voice as he was busily munching away. 'It makes you très hungry!'

'Très faim,' Tom corrected him.

'Tray famm,' Anna echoed. She was determined to learn some French words.

Silence reigned for a while as the food was demolished. Mum had to order in another round of croissants. Even then Kevin said he could still eat some more but Mum said she was worried he wouldn't fit through the car door.

'OK, Mrs D, better not risk it then!' he chuckled.

Mum smiled at his perennial good humour. He was a really cheerful kid, she thought. She was very fond of him. His parents were her best friends. Unfortunately, Kevin's Mum, Tanya, had multiple sclerosis and that was why Kevin usually came on holiday with the Donoghues. Tanya wanted Kevin to have active holidays which she couldn't manage any more. Mum marvelled at how Kevin stayed so cheerful with his mum so often very ill.

Tom was more moody than Kevin. Mum couldn't always predict how he'd react to being teased. Sometimes he'd be fine about it but at other times he wouldn't. He'd been a sunny, happy little boy but after Dad died, when he was seven, he'd become very withdrawn for a while. He'd taken it on himself to look after Mum and had become much more serious. Three years later, he was opening up again but Mum was aware he carried a heavy burden on his young shoulders.

Her glance fell on Anna, who was slowly but determinedly eating her way through a second croissant. Sadly, she'd never really known her father, which was a source of much sadness to

Mum. Mum knew she spoiled Anna sometimes but it was hard not to. The children had kept her going after her husband's death.

And there was Alan too, of course. They'd met Alan a year ago on their holiday in the Auvergne. He'd helped them escape an erupting volcano and since then he and Mum had become close friends. He'd joined them on their winter holiday in the French Alps last year, arriving just after Tom and Kevin had been caught in an avalanche. The two boys had then gone on to catch an explosives smuggler. Mum smiled as she thought how Alan would be coming to stay with them at the campsite in a week's time.

The rest of the day was spent travelling on the autoroutes. There were plenty of stops for food and drinks. Mum could only manage about two hours' driving at a time before she needed a break to relax. The children were glad to stretch their legs. Luckily all the service stations they stopped at had climbing frames and swings and things so they had a good run around.

At tea time they arrived at the hotel Mum had prebooked. The journey to the campsite was too long to do in one day.

'I think you'll like this hotel,' smiled Mum as she parked the car.

Kevin didn't look convinced. Tom looked intrigued.

'Why?' he asked.

'Because we've got a TV in the bedroom and there's an open air pool as well!' Mum announced triumphantly.

'Yippee for both!' yelled Kevin.

'What a cool hotel,' observed Tom. 'I thought hotels were pretty boring usually.'

'Well, this one isn't,' grinned Mum. 'Come on, bring your rucksacks and I'll dig the suitcases out of the boot.'

Their big family room was perfect — it opened straight out onto the pool area.

'Mega!' whooped Kevin.

He changed into his togs at lightning speed and sprinted to the pool. He stuck a foot in.

'Ow!' he shrieked. 'It's freezing!'

'Wimp,' teased Tom. 'I bet it's lovely.'

To show off he jumped straight in. Instantly he gave a great howl. All the others could see were threshing arms and legs as he struggled to the side and pulled himself out as quickly as possible.

'Oh boy, that was painful,' he groaned.

Anna and Kevin were laughing too much to say anything.

'It's not funny,' pouted Tom, sulking, but the laughter was infectious and he found himself joining in. 'I guess I must have looked pretty daft,' he admitted.

'Very daft,' Kevin corrected him. 'Come on, let's be brave and get in.'

But they hesitated for a minute. The water was freezing. To their surprise and shame, Mum beat them in. She appeared in her swimsuit, felt the water, winced slightly but dropped straight in.

'Lovely once you're in,' she told the boys and Anna. 'Come on you scaredy cats.'

'Mum's nerve endings must be dying off because she's old,' whispered Tom. 'That's why she doesn't feel the cold.'

'I heard that, young man,' Mum warned him. She splashed him in revenge. That got Tom in the water again. Once he was in, he splashed Kevin who jumped in beside him. Anna set her jaw and plopped straight in next to Mum.

They had a great half-hour, messing about in the water. It was so refreshing. But soon their rumbling tummies told them it was time to get out and find some tea.

'We could eat here in the restaurant,' said Mum hopefully, towelling her hair dry in their room.

'Er, actually, Mrs D, I caught sight of a McDonald's sign just before we pulled in to this hotel. It isn't far. I think we could walk.'

'Kevin Murphy!' laughed Mum. 'I think you could find a McDonald's on the moon. You must have some sort of inbuilt tracking system!'

'That's why he's my best friend!' smiled Tom. 'I couldn't possibly be friends with anyone who couldn't find a McDonald's anywhere, anytime.'

Kevin grinned broadly. 'I'm glad I'm useful!'

'OK, McDonald's it is,' sighed Mum. 'At least they do nice salads for me. I really fancied a beautiful salad niçoise though.' She looked wistful.

'I'm sure it's very fattening,' said Kevin. 'Not at all good for you. Not like a McDonald's salad!'

Mum threw a towel at him. 'Come on, then. You win,' she said. 'Let's go and eat.'

The children thundered to the door. Mum grabbed her handbag and hurried to catch them up.

2
The Campsite

It was about three o'clock the next afternoon when they arrived at the campsite at last. They'd long since left the autoroutes and for the last forty kilometres or so had been following small, winding roads.

'Just like being back in Ireland!' Tom had remarked.

Tom was in charge of map reading but he wasn't too good at it so they'd taken a few wrong turns. But at last here they were.

'Not a moment too soon!' exclaimed Mum, relieved. She was hot and sticky and dying for a cup of tea.

The campsite was on the edge of the small town of St Jean les Bains. It wasn't a very big campsite but it had its own snack bar and café. There was an adjoining playground with slides, swings and a climbing frame but best of all, the campsite was next to a river. An area of the water was marked out with floats for safe bathing. There were also canoes and kayaks to hire.

'You never said we were next to the river!'

yelped Tom in delight. 'Cool!'

'No, I didn't,' said Mum. 'I must have forgotten.' She winked at Kevin. 'Mind you,' she said, slightly anxiously, 'I hadn't actually realised we were quite this close! The river can only be about five metres from the campsite.'

'Great. Not too far to walk then,' observed Kevin.

'Well, put it like that and I have to agree,' smiled Mum. 'The bank slopes quite steeply so I suppose we're high enough above the river.' She felt uneasy though.

'Can we go in the canoes now, Mummy?' asked Anna.

'Goodness, not straight away, love!' exclaimed Mum. 'Let's unpack and have a drink first. Maybe we'll just paddle in the water tonight and save canoeing for tomorrow when we're fresh. How does that sound?'

It sounded very sensible to her ears but not to the children. However, Mum was firm. She was too tired for anything active today.

They called into the camp reception tent. The campsite manager showed them to their tent, which was surrounded by pine trees, right on the edge of the riverbank.

'One of the best spots, n'est-ce pas?' he smiled. Mum wasn't sure. The trees were nice but she would rather have been a bit further away from the water's edge.

The tent was quite luxurious. It had a cooking/dining area plus two separate bedrooms with zip-up walls. Mum and Anna would share one and Alan would have the other when he arrived next week. Outside was a much smaller tent that Mum had booked for the two boys to sleep in. This was another surprise for Tom and Kevin. They were thrilled.

'Great!' grinned Kevin. 'Now I won't have to wash my feet all week since they're not going to be under Mrs D's nose.'

'Yes you will,' Tom pointed out. 'Because they'll be under my nose. I'm sharing the tent too, you know.'

'Not if I don't wash my feet, you won't,' laughed his friend. 'I'll have the place to myself.'

Tom pulled a face. Mum left the children in the tent and went and fetched the car. There was a parking spot next to the tent. They soon unpacked all their stuff and had fun finding somewhere in the tent to put everything. Then they trooped off to the washrooms to freshen up.

Finally, Mum got her cup of tea at the snack bar. 'This is nice,' she sighed as they sat on the terrace, looking at the river flowing by. 'I purposely chose the quietest campsite I could find so we can be sure of a nice, peaceful holiday. But don't worry,' she added, seeing disapproval on the boys' faces, 'there are plenty of things to do around here. Starting tomorrow, you'll see.'

3
Canoe Trip

Ten o'clock next morning found them waiting outside the small hut that served as the booking office for the canoe hire company. A very hairy dog was waiting outside as well. Come quarter past ten they were still waiting.

Mum began to mutter crossly. 'It was meant to be open at ten. I don't know, I thought the French were always punctual.'

'Calm down, Mum,' soothed Tom. 'Someone will be here soon. Why don't you count fleas with Kev and me? Just watch that dog, he's crawling with them, poor thing.'

'Is he really?' said Mum, interested in spite of herself. 'Oh yes, I see one on his head, no two. Gosh, they must be itchy.'

'I can see three on his tail!' squeaked Anna.

They were so engrossed that they were taken by surprise when the hut door suddenly swung open. A young, tanned man had just unlocked it from inside.

'Je m'excuse,' he smiled, looking not the slightest bit sorry. 'Monday mornings, I can never get up! Now, you want canoes, yes?'

'Please,' nodded Mum. 'Two two-seaters. We'll be going as far as Lucville. What time will you pick us up from there?'

'The minibus will be there at one o'clock. This is plenty of time to arrive,' the man informed them.

Mum paid and then they went down to the river's edge where they got their canoes, paddles, life-jackets and a big plastic barrel called a bidon to put their things in. Mum dropped their shoes and her bag in and screwed the lid down tight.

'That should keep the water out!'

'Actually, you don't need a lid, Mum,' said Tom. 'The smell of Kevin's shoes will keep the water out!'

Mum was slightly concerned that they weren't given helmets, especially as the riverbed was very rocky.

'Don't worry about us,' said Kevin. 'Our heads are mega hard. We're always hitting them but never feel a thing.'

Mum smiled. 'Yes, I expect I'm being fussy. I have to admit, it's nicer without a sticky helmet on.'

'There you are, then,' said Tom. 'We're all happier without them. Come on, let's go!'

He and Kevin shared one canoe while Mum and Anna had the other. Anna sat in the front of that one.

She had a plastic mini-paddle so she could 'help' Mum. Every time she stuck it in the river, though, she showered Mum with water and made the canoe go wonky. But Mum didn't mind. It was lovely to be gliding along the shallow water.

The boys took a little while to get used to controlling the canoe. To start with they both paddled on the same side which meant the canoe veered off in one direction. So, to correct it, they started paddling on that side, and of course the canoe veered off in the other direction! They accused each other noisily of causing the problem but soon got the hang of things . . . more or less.

After a while they came to an old, low bridge, covered thickly with ivy. Mum and Anna admired it but the boys were too busy peering into the water. Tom just gave it a quick glance as they paddled underneath it.

'Hey,' called Kevin suddenly. 'Look at these huge fish. Are they sharks?'

The others peered into the clear water. It was true! The fish – Tom reckoned they were trout – were enormous and quite vicious looking. Anna, who had been trailing her hand in the water, quickly pulled it out.

'Don't worry,' smiled Mum. 'They won't hurt

you. It's those sort of bristly things on their head that make them look fierce, isn't it? I'd love some trout with almonds at a nice restaurant sometime during this holiday.'

'You mean McDonald's don't do trout?' gasped Kevin in mock surprise.

'No,' said Mum. 'Now watch it guys, a rough patch ahead. Aim between those rocks, OK?'

Sure enough the water was boiling in front of them. Anna squealed and held onto the sides of the canoe tightly. Mum paddled frantically to keep the canoe on the right course for shooting through the gap in the rocks, and then shouted 'Whee!' as the current suddenly gripped the canoe and propelled it along.

'Here goes!' called Tom nervously. He was sitting in the front and felt very exposed. He tried to follow Mum's path but the rough water pushed them to one side. They bounced off the first rock and scraped along the side of the second before bobbing along in the current after Mum.

'Phew! Thank goodness these canoes are tough!' exclaimed Kevin. 'Rotten steering by the way, Tom!'

Tom replied by splashing Kevin, who retaliated in kind. Soon they were both soaking.

There were several more dodgy patches to get through. Mum managed them effortlessly but the boys were pretty hopeless. They hit a good few rocks and took on a lot of water.

'Can we pull in for a minute, Mum?' called Tom. 'Me and Kev have got half the river in our canoe. I think we'd better let the fish have it back.'

'Of course,' replied Mum. 'My arms are beginning to ache. Look, there's a nice gravel bank over there. That's a good place to stop.'

A few minutes later they glided onto the bank. Mum helped the boys empty their canoe out. She was astonished at the quantity of water inside.

'Any more and you'd have sunk,' she teased.

Mum opened the bidon and pulled out some cans of Orangina and an assortment of bars from her bag.

'Not quite as nice as a café au lait and an éclair au chocolat, but not bad,' she admitted as they lounged in the sun, eating and drinking happily.

'Much better than coffee and cakes,' Tom teased.

'Yes, Mrs D, and much healthier too,' added Kevin seriously. 'You shouldn't have too much caffeine, you know, it's not good for you. Too much makes people jittery, or so my dad says.'

'But not as jittery as too much Kevin,' grinned Tom.

Anna giggled in delight.

'Hey, Annie, I thought you were my friend,' said Kevin, pretending to be upset.

'Come on,' sighed Mum, sitting up. 'We'd better carry on. I reckon we're about halfway to Lucville. We don't want to miss our ride home.'

4
Stuck

Their arms complained for the next few hundred metres of rowing but after that they loosened up again. Gradually the river began to change. It got narrower and rockier. The banks, which had been low and grassy, became high and craggy. The water was choppier.

'I'm not sure I like this,' muttered Kevin to himself as they narrowly missed hitting the base of a bridge as the river whisked them through. But Tom seemed to be enjoying himself, and Mum and Anna certainly were. I must be more of a wimp than I realised, he thought. So he put on a show of enjoying himself.

But soon the two canoes were careering towards what looked like a solid wall of boulders across the river. The water swirled and boiled.

'Follow me!' called Mum, and aimed her canoe at a small gap between the rocks. She zoomed through deftly.

The boys hoped for the best. They hadn't been very good at steering in the calmer parts so they both knew they hadn't got a hope here. Tom managed to turn the front of the canoe more or less towards the gap Mum had gone through. But at the last minute a swirl of water lifted the canoe and then plonked it down firmly in another, much smaller gap between two rocks. The canoe came to a bumpy halt.

Kevin gave up any pretence of being cool.

'We're stuck!' he cried.

They were. Well and truly stuck between two large rocks in the middle of the river. The water gushed and whirled around them.

'Do something, Tom!' yelled Kevin, starting to panic. He wasn't too keen on swimming, especially in a shallow, rocky torrent.

Tom prodded ineffectually at the rocks beside them but the canoe didn't budge. Seconds later the water ripped the paddle out of his hands.

'Oh no!' he howled. 'Mum! Mum! Help!'

Mum was a good way down the river, riding the current. She didn't hear him but luckily she checked over her shoulder to see how the boys were doing.

'Oh Anna, they're stuck,' she shouted above the noise of the water.

'Mummy, there's Tom's paddle.' Anna pointed at the bright yellow object coming towards them. Mum tried desperately to turn the canoe to intercept it but couldn't do it. The paddle swirled by.

'Never mind, let's try and help the boys,' said Mum.

She began paddling back upriver towards them but it was tough going. The river was flowing too fast.

'We'll have to pull into the bank and I'll walk back,' Mum decided as she headed for shore.

Meanwhile, Tom was still trying to get them free. He could see that Kevin had totally lost it. His friend was gripping the sides of the canoe, rigid with fear.

'Stay cool, Kev!' yelled Tom. 'We'll get out of here in a minute.'

But he wasn't sure how. He'd tried rocking the canoe by swaying from side to side but that hadn't done any good. Then he'd tried tilting it by sliding his weight down to the nose of the canoe. But suddenly he'd got scared that they might tip over so he pushed his weight back nearer the middle. He hoped the water might push them out of the gap but so far it hadn't. And the constant roar of the river was getting to him. There was no way either of them could climb out of the canoe. It would be mad to do so — their feet would be knocked from under them instantly by the force of the water. Tom shuddered as he thought about being thrown onto the jagged rocks around them.

He was relieved to see Mum hurrying along the bank towards them. She was shouting to them but Tom couldn't hear a word. Soon Mum was level with them. She made swaying movements to tell Tom to rock the canoe. He knew it was hopeless but he did it anyway. Mum began to wave her arms but Tom couldn't make out what she was trying to tell him.

'Do you know what Mum's saying?' he called to Kevin. Kevin looked at him blankly in terror.

Then Mum picked up a large branch lying nearby and started to try and wade out towards the boys.

'Don't Mum,' yelled Tom. 'You'll get hurt!'

Mum didn't hear him but she soon realised that there was no way she'd get to the boys. The water was ripping at her feet already even though she was only a few paces out from the river's edge. It was no good getting herself knocked unconscious or drowned. That would be of no help to anyone. She reluctantly turned back to the shore. She decided she would fetch Anna from the canoe where she'd left her, with strict warnings to sit still, and return to wait by the boys. When they didn't arrive at the pick-up point at Lucville, surely the trip organisers would come looking for them and rescue Tom and Kevin.

'Why is life never simple?' muttered Mum crossly.

Tom was getting panicky now. The constant noise of the water was really unnerving. And he could see that Kevin was in tears. Things looked black. But then he quickly pulled himself together. There must be a scientific way of getting out of this mess. And Tom prided himself on being good at science. It was his favourite subject at school. And Dad had been a brilliant scientist, Mum said. She was always telling him that he took after his father.

'What would you have done, Dad?' he wondered. Then, quite suddenly, he saw what the problem was.

'Kev, come on, you've got to help me or we'll be stuck here forever,' he shouted. 'Wriggle towards me. You're sitting over the point where we're stuck. If we can move your weight away from there, we might get free.'

Kevin didn't budge.

'Kev, come on.'

Still no response. It wasn't that Kevin couldn't hear Tom, it was just that he couldn't move. He was too scared to budge.

'Kev, please,' begged Tom. 'Come on, buddy, we're a team. Trust me, Kev, we'll be OK. We won't fall in. Besides I don't want to spend all our holiday here. No burgers if we do!'

The magic word 'burgers' broke through Kevin's fear at last. He looked up. Tom was right — he had to do something to help. Slowly Kevin loosened his grip on the sides of the canoe. He tried not to let his eyes stray onto the rocks all around them.

'Atta boy!' shouted Tom. 'Now, wriggle forwards, just a bit.'

Kevin slid his bottom forward a little way. The canoe shifted in response. Kevin froze again.

'Hooray! It moved. Try again,' urged Tom.

Kevin took a deep breath and wriggled just a little bit further. Suddenly it felt like he was falling as the canoe slid out of its perch and splashed free into the river. The boys were whirled round and round as the canoe spun wildly in the water — but at least they didn't capsize. Mum and Anna watched anxiously from the bank.

Then Kevin remembered about his paddle. For some reason it was lying next to him in his section of the canoe. Kevin had no idea how it had got there.

He shoved it into the water and dragged on it to slow them down and stop them spinning.

'Good work, Kev,' called Tom, when at last the canoe was back under control. Admittedly they were now floating backwards down the river but the ordeal was over.

'Give me your paddle and I'll get us to the bank,' said Tom. 'You must be exhausted.'

Kevin was, and he was still pretty dazed so he happily let Tom manoeuvre them carefully to shore. When they got there Kevin climbed out shakily. Mum enveloped him in a big hug. Kevin sobbed gratefully. Tom felt close to tears too. Mum found an arm to put round him as well while Anna watched solemnly.

'Well done, guys,' said Mum. 'You were very brave.'

'I wasn't,' sniffed Kevin. 'I was useless.'

'No you weren't,' said Tom loyally. 'You kept hold of your paddle and it was you who got us free in the end. And you stopped us going round in circles.'

'Superman look out,' said Kevin, managing a watery smile.

'That's our Kevin,' grinned Mum, giving him a last hug. 'Now, if I remember rightly there were a couple of bars left in the bidon. I think we all need a burst of sugar to calm our nerves, eh? We've all had a nasty fright.'

They munched in silence then reluctantly climbed back into the canoes. Mum explained to the others that there was no other way to get to Lucville.

'Look,' she announced, 'if we see any more rough, rocky patches, we'll head for the shore and either paddle along there or, if necessary, we can get out and drag the canoes along. We don't need to shoot any more rapids. How does that sound?'

'Fine,' said Tom. Kevin just nodded. He still felt wobbly and didn't trust himself to speak very much.

So they set off slowly. With only one paddle, the boys couldn't go fast. But not much further downriver Anna spotted a flash of yellow among some reeds in the shallow water at the river's edge.

'Tom's paddle!' she squealed.

'Where?' asked Mum. 'Oh yes, I see it. Well done, Anna!'

Tom sighed with relief. Now no one else need ever know what had happened to him and Kevin. It would have been embarrassing owning up to the canoe hire people that they'd got stuck on the rocks and lost a paddle as a result. Mum retrieved it and they continued uneventfully on their journey. The minibus was there to meet them at Lucville. Tom was a bit disappointed about that. Their eventful journey down the river ended at a large dam-like structure with a tall building beside it. Tom would have loved to explore it, but there clearly wasn't time today. Plus the others looked too tired to care.

'Bonjour! Did you have a good trip?' asked the driver as he loaded the canoes up on the trailer behind the bus.

'It's a lovely river,' replied Mum, vaguely.

But Kevin wasn't sure he even agreed with that answer.

5
A Cycle Ride

Pizza and chips at the campsite café for lunch restored Kevin's spirits. Soon he was chatting happily about what else they could do that week.

'Lot's of cycling please, Mrs D,' he pleaded. 'It's so lovely and sunny. It's nearly always too wet to do much cycling back home.'

'Yes, can we go for a ride this afternoon, Mum?' asked Tom.

'Well,' said Mum, 'I was going to go shopping.'

'Oh no!' groaned Kevin and Tom in unison.

'But since it's such lovely weather and since I can't really be bothered, then yes, let's go cycling,' Mum continued.

'Cool!' grinned Kevin.

'I'll have to get some stuff from the épicerie in the village when we get back otherwise we'll have nothing for tea. I'm afraid we can't afford to eat out every mealtime,' sighed Mum.

'Just get lots of chips and burgers, then please,' said Tom.

Mum pulled a face. 'We'll see. But I might get one or two things that are just a tiny bit healthier.'

'Nothing's healthier than chips,' muttered Kevin. Mum pretended not to hear.

'Where shall we cycle to then?' asked Tom.

Mum pulled out a map and spread it on the café table, after shooing away a very insistent wasp with it first.

'I think we'll stick to flat ground today after our exertions this morning,' she suggested. 'We'll tackle the hills another day. I noticed something interesting on the map when I was looking at it last night. Now, where was it? I thought I'd marked it.' Mum frowned and peered at the map. 'Aha, there we are,' she said pointing to a ring in blue biro. 'It says source. That means 'spring'. There used to be thermal baths at this town many years ago. That's why it has les bains in its name.'

'What are thermal baths?' asked Kevin. 'They sound a bit too clean for my liking!'

'Thermal baths are where naturally warm water comes to the surface,' Tom explained. He was the scientist after all. 'Often the water has something special about it too, like lots of sulphur or iron in it. That can be good for your health.'

'It can?' Kevin was sceptical.

'People used to go to thermal baths and drink the water or sit in it, but not at the same time I don't think!' Tom smiled, quite pleased with himself.

'That's right,' said Mum. 'People still go to thermal baths these days. But they're not as popular as they used to be and there aren't so many around. The one here at St Jean les Bains was very big once. Some of the kings of France even came here.'

'Mega! Perhaps one of the kings lost his crown here or something and we might find it.' Kevin rubbed his hands at the prospect.

'Don't be dumb,' said Tom. 'Kings didn't go around losing crowns. They had too many servants looking after them. They probably never lost anything.'

'Unlike some,' said Mum, looking at Tom. Tom pulled a face. He was the world's worst at losing stuff. Well, he usually found it again, or rather Mum usually found it again . . . eventually. 'Tom spends a lot of time looking for things he's left in weird places.'

'Get him a servant then, Mrs D,' suggested Kevin.

'He doesn't need one, he's got me! Anyway, we'd better get going, or we won't get far on our bikes before tea time.'

Mum paid the waitress and then they all went back to the tent. They changed into cycling gear and

Mum checked the bikes' tyres. Before they'd left home she'd had to let some air out before putting them on the bike carriers on the roof of the car. Now they were much too soft for cycling. Tom and Kevin pumped like crazy to inflate them again.

'That should do,' said Mum, squeezing the last tyre. 'Nice and hard.'

'Thank goodness,' panted Tom. 'Pumping is jolly hard work. I'm nearly too tired to cycle now!'

'Weakling!' teased Kevin. 'I could pump up a million more tyres and then cycle a trillion miles.'

'When you two have quite finished,' said Mum, sounding very much like their teacher, 'let's go!'

They set off, at first on the wrong side of the road until Mum saw a car coming towards them and remembered where they were meant to be. They quickly swerved across to the right hand side.

'Whoops!' said Mum. 'Not a good start!'

But Anna didn't care. She was really enjoying the ride. Now that she was four, she had a small trailer bike that fitted onto the back of Mum's mountain bike, turning it into a sort of tandem. She could pedal away when she wanted or just sit on the saddle and enjoy the ride. It was much better than being stuck in the child seat that she used to have. The trailer bike was very unusual and passers-by always turned to stare and wave. Anna loved the attention and grinned happily back.

Tom and Kevin raced each other, stopping every now and again to let Mum catch up. They didn't have to wait too long — Mum was very fit and, as Kevin said, she was a mean cyclist. So they soon covered a fair bit of ground.

'We need to look for a track going off to the right fairly soon now,' said Mum, checking the map when they next stopped for a breather. 'I expect it will be a bit rough but we should be able to cycle it.' They all had good mountain bikes.

Tom and Kevin scouted ahead. They found a sandy track on their right and began to cycle along it but when they turned a corner they saw a farmyard in front of them. A big dog barked and ran towards them.

'Quick, scarper!' yelled Tom. They zoomed back to the road, just in time to stop Mum from turning onto the track too.

'Not this one,' called Kevin, not stopping to explain but charging off down the road, closely followed by Tom. Mum looked puzzled for a second but then she saw the dog bounding along. She zipped off after the boys. The dog chased them half-heartedly for a little way. Anna thought it was brilliant although she did lift her legs up out of nipping range.

The next track looked more hopeful. It didn't lead to a farm and an angry dog, but into a nice shady wood, which came as a welcome relief after the baking roads they'd been on up till now.

'What are we looking for exactly, Mum?' asked Tom. They had stopped for a drink from their water bottles.

'I'm not really sure,' Mum admitted. 'Just some sort of spring, maybe like the holy well at St Gobnait's.'

'Oh, what's that?' asked Kevin. He'd never been there.

'It's in a wood we go walking in sometimes,' Tom told him. 'You go through a churchyard and down the road there's this well. It's a bit like a little shrine I suppose and there are these really old cups you can use to drink the water. Only Mum doesn't let us use them 'cos she says we might get germs. So we use our hands.'

'Personally I'd rather risk the cup,' said Kevin with a grin.

'But maybe it'll be more like a cave or a fountain here,' said Mum. 'Just keep a look out for anything strange.'

6
Orange Mud

They heard the spring before they saw it. They hadn't cycled far after their last break when they heard the sound of splashing water. It was coming from the woods to the left of them.

'Let's leave the bikes and investigate,' said Mum.

Setting off on foot, they pushed their way through some brambles and undergrowth, following the sound. The earth, they noticed, was very red, in fact almost orange. They scrambled down a muddy bank and then, quite suddenly, found the source. What a disappointment! Instead of an ornate shrine or a mysterious cavern there was just a very rusty pipe sticking up out of the ground and reddish-brown water was splashing out of it.

'Yuck!' said Kevin, speaking for all of them.

'Are you going to try the water?' Tom asked Mum.

'No! Come on, this wasn't worth the effort was it?' she sighed.

They got back to their bikes with a good few bramble scratches on their legs.

'Do you want to head back or explore a bit further?' asked Mum.

'Bit further,' said Tom and Anna.

'Go back,' said Kevin.

'Sorry, Kevin, I want to go on too so you're outvoted,' smiled Mum.

'You Donoghues are just conspiring against me,' replied Kevin. But he didn't mind being overruled.

They set off again. Then Tom gave a shout.

'Look! A sign! It says "La source", I think.'

He was right. A small, tatty sign, half hidden by brambles, pointed down to the left.

'Do you think it's pointing back to that pipe we saw?' asked Kevin.

Mum looked into the woods. 'I don't think so,' she said, hopefully. 'The path seems to lead away from the pipe. Let's just have a quick look, OK?'

Tom and Kevin didn't really want to get scratched by brambles again, but they didn't want to disappoint Mum. She clearly wanted to see if this source was better than the last one. Leaving their bikes once more they went to investigate. They scrabbled through the trees, following the narrow path. Kevin took the lead. He pushed through a thick bush of brambles then suddenly gave a yell and disappeared from sight. There was a loud, splotchy noise.

'Kev, are you OK?' called Tom, hurrying forward.

'Yeah, but watch it, there's a big drop!'

Tom heard the warning just in time. Peering through the brambles, he saw the path suddenly ending. It started again about a metre lower, currently underneath where Kevin was lying. It also became very, very muddy. The mud was a bright orangey-red colour, like the colour of the spring water they'd seen earlier. Kevin was covered in mud.

'Crikey, Mum will have a million fits when she sees you,' grinned Tom. 'She didn't want to have to do much washing this holiday. You're filthy!'

Kevin pulled himself up. His feet disappeared into the orange sludge.

'But hey, I've found something! There's a tunnel here! It's full of mud though. Maybe it leads to the source. Tell your mum.'

Mum and Anna had caught up with Tom by now. Tom quickly filled her in on what Kevin had found.

What's the tunnel like, Kevin?' she asked.

'It's lined with brick. And there seems to be a pipe running along one side. Not sure why though.

It's very dark, but I think it's quite long. Looks like it slopes upwards too. Have you got a torch, Mrs D?' Kevin reappeared out of the tunnel entrance.

Mum gasped when she saw him. 'Good grief, you've turned orange, Kevin Murphy!'

'True, but I bet I've found that source you're looking for!' Kevin looked triumphant. 'We really need a torch though.'

'Hang on, I've got one in the pannier on my bike,' Tom remembered. 'Will I get it, Mum?'

'Yes please. I'd like to have a look in Kevin's tunnel. It sounds interesting.'

Tom zoomed back to his bike. Mum gingerly lowered herself down to join Kevin. She grimaced as her feet disappeared in the soft, orange mud.

'Yuck!'

Then she helped Anna drop down. Anna was thrilled with the mud. It was great Mum not minding her stomping around in it. Mum could be a bit of a spoilsport sometimes where mud was concerned.

Thudding footsteps announced Tom's return. He plopped down beside them and shone his torch into the tunnel entrance. It was impressive, about two metres tall and a metre wide. It was carved out of the rock, but as Kevin had said, it was lined with brick. The structure seemed to be pretty old.

'Stay here while I have a quick poke around,' ordered Mum.

Kevin groaned. 'Oh, you get all the fun things to do,' he moaned, 'like drive the car, and tell Tom off and go into tunnels first!'

'True,' smiled Mum, 'but I also get to do all the not-so-fun things like wash dirty socks, cook endless meals for you lot and pay bills. So I deserve the first look in the tunnel!'

'Well, if you put it like that,' shrugged Kevin, who didn't mind Mum going first really as the tunnel was very dark.

Mum squelched her way into the tunnel. She got ten metres or so before she needed to put the torch on. She shone it in front of her. The tunnel was very long and steeply sloping.

'I'll go a bit further, guys!' she called back. She trudged on, banging her head a couple of times on the roof. 'Ouch!' she said crossly after a particularly hard knock. All at once, whirring wings surrounded her as small black bodies whizzed round her head. She screamed in surprise.

'Mum! Mum! Are you OK?' shouted Tom, who'd heard the shriek.

The bats had fluttered off by now.

'Yes, I'm fine. Sorry love! I surprised some bats

— and they surprised me!'

'Bats? Mega cool!' gasped Kevin. 'Can I come and see them?'

'They've flown off, I'm afraid. No, hold on, there are some hanging from the roof.' Mum swept the tunnel ceiling with torchlight. 'Come and have a look!'

She shone the torch back down the tunnel so the children could see their way to reach her. Tom held Anna's hand and they followed Kevin as far as Mum. Tom felt a thrill of excitement as he crept along inside the tunnel. This was really cool, like smugglers or something, he thought.

They gazed at all the bats hanging from the roof.

'They look like mice!' squeaked Anna.

'And you sound like one!' teased Tom.

'Do you know what the French call bats?' asked Mum.

'Les bats?' hazarded Kevin.

'Chauves souris,' Mum told them. 'Which means 'bald mice'!'

'Hey, I like that,' said Kevin. 'I mean, they really are bald mice, aren't they. Just upside down bald mice with wings!'

'Come on, let's go a bit further down the tunnel,' begged Tom. 'Can we, Mum?'

Mum flashed the torch in front of her. The tunnel walls looked good and solid. 'OK, I don't see why not. Here, you'd better take the torch.'

'Wicked!' grinned Tom, heading off first and quickly followed by Kevin.

They plodded through the deep mud. Anna held on very tightly to Mum's hand. She wasn't keen on going further, but she was determined to keep up with the boys. Mum wasn't that enthusiastic either, but didn't want the boys to think she was boring. She didn't want them to miss out on some fun either. This was a real adventure for them.

'Mum, Mum!' called Tom, 'I think I can see daylight ahead!'

'Really? How far away?'

'Not so far, about twenty metres maybe?' Tom actually didn't have a clue about the distance but twenty metres sounded about right.

'Go on then,' said Mum, 'but be careful.'

Tom hurried forward, Kevin breathing down his neck. Yes, it was definitely daylight. Tom turned his torch off. There was just enough light to see his way. He pushed on towards the end of the tunnel.

He came blinking into the sunlight, not in another part of the wood as he expected, but in the bottom of a deep gully. A small waterfall trickled down one side, and thick creepers grew all around. The ground was boggy and still that bright orange colour.

'Wow!' Kevin emerged to join his friend. 'Whatever is this?' He gazed around in surprise.

Mum and Anna had arrived by now.

'This is fun!' exclaimed Mum. 'We've found a secret chamber.'

'Really?' gasped Anna, eyes wide with wonder.

'Definitely,' nodded Kevin. 'The only way in is through that tunnel and I bet hardly anyone knows about it. I reckon those guard bats see most people off.'

One side of the gully was less steep than the others.

'I reckon we could climb up there,' said Tom, pointing.

'Probably,' Mum agreed, 'but not today. It's still a steep climb and we've already done a lot of exploring. And don't forget, we've got to go all the way back.'

Tom looked disappointed.

'We'll come again another day. And we'll bring Alan. He'd love this!' Mum told him.

'OK,' Tom nodded. 'You promise?'

'I promise.'

7
The Barrage

'All set to go home?' asked Mum, once they were back at the bikes

'How far is Lucville?' asked Tom.

'Crikey, about a million kilometres, isn't it?' Kevin looked dismayed. 'At least, that's what it felt like when we canoed there.'

'Let's see,' said Mum, unfolding the map and peering at it. 'The river bends a lot, much more than the road in the valley. So it won't be as far cycling as it was canoeing. Why do you want to go to Lucville, Tom?'

'Well, remember the dam and the building there? I'd like to have a closer look.'

'Was there a dam?' asked Mum. 'Gosh, I don't think it registered. I was so weary, not to mention also a nervous wreck at the end of our fun-filled journey down the river!'

'Huh, some fun!' protested Kevin. 'I don't remember a dam either. I think Tom's making it up!'

'You guys just go around with your eyes shut,' observed Tom. 'Is there a dam on the map, Mum?'

'Hang on. Where are we? Oh, yes, here. Well,

yes there is something across the river. It's marked as "barrage".'

'See?' Tom was triumphant.

Kevin grinned. 'That's our Tom. Eagle-eyed as ever!'

'Oh, there are quite a few barrages actually,' said Mum, studying the map with interest. 'Hey, there's a small one not far from the campsite, just upriver from it. That one's a lot nearer than Lucville. How about we go there? It seems to be in the middle of nowhere. Which is probably just as well — we're all very muddy, especially one of us,' she winked at Kevin. 'We might put the people of Lucville off their dinners.'

'Knowing the French, unlikely,' announced Tom. 'They love their food. All they seem to do is eat.'

'Which is why France is the perfect country for me to bring you and Kevin to,' smiled Mum.

'Just healthy appetites,' nodded Kevin. 'Which reminds me, I'm hungry.'

'Oh, you can't be, surely!' sighed Mum. 'Look, let's see this barrage, then when we get back I'll buy you each an ice cream from the campsite café.'

'Done!' cried Kevin and Tom together.

'Two ice creams please,' demanded Anna.

'OK,' smiled Mum. 'Two ice creams for you.' She saw the boy's jealous faces. 'And you too, so long as you're not sick in the tent afterwards!'

'I'm never sick,' announced Kevin, proudly.

'Liar,' Tom butted in. 'You were sick in my sleeping bag at your house once. And I was still lying in it, remember? You'd had about a hundred helpings of toffee pudding for tea and . . .' he trailed off, aware of Mum's horrified stare.

'Um, didn't I ever tell you about that, Mum?'

Mum shook her head. 'No you didn't. And I'm not sure I really want to know now either.' She pulled a face. 'Yuk! Anyway, that's enough of that. Let's go to our barrage!'

They mounted the bikes and pedalled off enthusiastically. All three children were trying to decide what ice creams they'd have. French ice creams were much nicer than the ones they got at home. Much more expensive too, as Mum was always pointing out. But she still bought them and Tom happened to know she enjoyed them just as much as the rest of them. Especially those choc-ices with the white chocolate and almond coating. Come to think of it, Tom thought those were pretty mega as well. He realised his mouth was watering at the thought!

The ride was a bit further than they'd all hoped but at last the road rounded a bend and there was the barrage stretching across the river, like a wide, solid bridge. It was surprisingly large and a road went over it. They cycled onto it and peered down over the side. They could just see some big metal sluice gates below them, regulating the flow of the water. Somewhere beneath them too they could hear the chug of machinery. On the left bank of the river was a small building.

'What is it? I mean, what's this barrage for?' asked Kevin, puzzled.

'Is it for hydroelectricity?' hazarded Tom.

Mum looked thoughtful for a moment as she looked at the construction. Then her face cleared. 'I know! You're almost right, Tom. It's actually a tidal power station, rather than a hydroelectric one. Hydroelectricity works using the power of water falling from a height to make turbines turn and generate electricity. Tidal power uses the power of the tide going in and out along the river. I remember reading about it on the Internet when I was finding out about this area. When a high tide comes in, water flows up the river and through tunnels in the barrage where the turbines are to make electricity. They'll be underneath us. Then the big sluice gate is lowered to capture the incoming water. At low tide, the gate is raised and the water flows out, making the turbines turn again. They're two-way turbines you see.'

'Cool!' observed Kevin.

'So it's renewable energy then?' asked Tom.

'Yes,' said Mum. 'No greenhouse gases, no nuclear waste — very clean! Plus the sluice gate helps control storm surges in bad weather.'

'But the turbines don't produce electricity all the time, though, do they? Only when the tide is going in or out,' said Tom thoughtfully.

'That's true,' agreed Mum. 'They can probably only generate power for ten or so hours a day. But that's still a fair amount of power.'

'Is there one in Ireland?' asked Anna.

'Golly, no idea,' admitted Mum. 'I'll have to look that up on the Internet when we get home.'

'You're not starting to get computer withdrawal symptoms are you, Mum?' grinned Tom.

'Well, just a tiny bit,' confessed Mum, who loved computers and everything to do with them. 'I'll get by though!'

They looked back down over the barrage admiringly for a few minutes. Then they turned and looked upriver. There was a quarry a kilometre or so away. Sounds of crunching machinery floated towards them, as did a lot of dust. There was a huge heap of rocks close to the river's edge.

'Bit of an eyesore,' remarked Mum.

'Yeah, and the rotten dust is making my eyes sore too!' quipped Kevin, rubbing his left eye.

'Don't rub it,' Anna told him bossily. 'Just blink.'

Kevin looked at her in surprise.

'That's what I tell her to do,' laughed Mum. 'Anna's just passing on sound advice.'

'Look, campers!' said Anna suddenly, pointing to a collection of rather shabby-looking tents on the far side of the river, close to the barrage. No one had spotted them before. A group of campers was sitting on the grass. One of them was very striking looking. He had a huge bushy red beard and just as much curly red hair.

'Funny campers,' mused Kevin. 'They've got signs up, see?'

It was true. There were some large white posters close to the tents.

'Non aux barrages,' read Tom. 'What does that mean, Mum?' asked Tom.

Mum shrugged. 'Simply "No to dams".' These people seem to be protesting against the barrages.

Any sort of dam like this does have an ecological effect, of course. Some birds and animals lose their habitats, and fish can get trapped in the turbines, although you see that little chute there, on the right hand side of the main sluice gates?' Mum pointed. 'I reckon that's a fish run.'

'Wouldn't they have to be real brainbox fish to find that chute thing, though? And know what it's for?' demanded Kevin.

'I really don't know, Kevin,' shrugged Mum. 'I guess plenty of fish must make it through safely.'

'So they're ecoterrorists then,' said Tom, returning to the campers. 'Or is it ecowarriors, I can never remember.'

'They both sound fierce,' said Kevin. 'Are they baddies?'

'I'm sure they're neither terrorists nor warriors,' said Mum, 'just people protesting peacefully to make their views known.'

'If I was them, I'd moan about the quarry, not the barrage. I think the barrage is cool,' said Tom.

'Do you think these ecoterrorist guys might blow the barrage up or something?' asked Kevin hopefully.

'Goodness, no! Well, I hope not,' said Mum. 'You've got an overactive imagination, young man.'

'Nah, he just plays too many violent games on his Playstation,' explained Tom. 'It's made him weird.'

'Not half as weird as you!' retorted Kevin.

'Rubbish, I'm not weird—'

'Enough!' Mum interrupted them. 'Come on, time to head back. Remember those ice creams I promised!'

'Yippee! Ice creams!' The boys forgot their argument at once and all four of them cycled energetically back to the campsite.

8
Rain

That was the last fine day. Next morning it began to rain. At first it was quite fun, wandering around in their kagoules and soggy sandals. But after a whole day of it, everything in the tent was starting to feel damp. The sleeping bags felt clammy. Tom and Kevin moved into the big tent. Their little one wasn't waterproof at all. Mum went to complain to the campsite manager. He shrugged apologetically and admitted the tents weren't designed to withstand heavy rains. A night's dew was their limit. Mum tut-tutted crossly and they squelched back to the tent.

'Let's hope it will be dry tomorrow,' sighed Mum as she tucked the boys and Anna in.

But all night long the rain drummed against the canvas of the tent. Pools of water collected underneath the doorway and in odd corners of the bedroom area. The tent was a thoroughly miserable place to be the next morning.

'Brr, it's chilly,' shivered Mum over breakfast. Even mugs of hot tea didn't warm them up.

'Mummy, why is it raining?' asked Anna

suddenly. 'It's not meant to rain on holiday, is it?'

'No, it isn't,' replied Kevin firmly. 'Mrs D, kindly tell the rain it isn't meant to fall!'

Mum smiled. 'I'll try, if you like.' She looked out of the plastic front door. 'Rain, stop!' she ordered sternly.

Anna giggled. 'It's still raining!'

'That's because Mum didn't say it in French. This is French rain, remember,' said Tom.

'Crikey, what would that be in French?' Mum wondered. 'Rain is pluie I think, but I'm not sure what the verb is. I always get it muddled up with pleurer, which is to cry. Let me think, what can I say?'

Mum frowned. The others waited expectantly.

'Got it,' Mum beamed. 'Pluie, arrêtez!'

'Pluie, arrêtez!' chanted the others. 'Pluie, arrêtez! Pluie, arrêtez!'

But it kept on raining.

'So what will we do this morning, Mum?' asked Tom. They'd been planning a long cycle ride but that didn't seem very appealing now.

'Well, we've got to collect Alan from the airport this afternoon. We might as well head into the city now and spend the morning there. I'm sick of feeling damp,' sighed Mum. 'Besides, there's plenty

to see there. There's a cathedral and an art museum
. . .'

Kevin groaned.

'. . . and probably a McDonald's.'

Kevin grinned.

'Can we go to a hypermarché?' begged Tom. The only time he enjoyed shopping was when they went to one of the huge French supermarkets.

'Yes please!' added Anna. Both she and Tom knew that Mum loved hypermarchés every bit as much as they did and that she would buy them all sorts of treats since lots of things were cheaper than at home.

So, breakfast over, they put on damp clothes, damp sandals and damp kagoules and drove to the city. Mum put the heater on in the car to try and dry their feet out. It was boiling hot but no one objected. It was far better than being cold and damp.

Mum found somewhere to park surprisingly easily. Usually it was a bit of a nightmare going into the cities. Mum would be trying to map read and drive at the same time while the boys and Anna would be looking out for parking signs, but never quite seeing them until it was too late. Mum usually got cross. But today they sailed into a huge car park with no problem at all.

'I like this place!' grinned Mum.

And so did the children, apart from the rain, of course. They only had a quick look in the cathedral, to Tom's relief, and the art museum was closed for some reason, to Kevin's relief. So they pottered around the shops with plenty of stops for Oranginas and pastries before driving off to the outskirts of the city to a hypermarché.

It was brilliant. They cruised up and down the endless aisles, cooing over the fabulous selection of goods. It was a good two hours later when they re-emerged into the rain with a trolley full to bursting point with just about everything. Anna hadn't found the Furby she was looking for so she'd settled for a Little Pony instead. Tom and Kevin got some Action Man accessories.

Kevin had chosen a raft. 'Action Man really needs it in this weather,' he joked. Tom chose a camping set for his Action Man with a tent, sleeping bag and rucksack full of knives, plates and things.

Mum had opted for some clothes and smelly stuff as well as vast quantities of delicious food 'Some good food will make up for the rotten weather,' she told them. Well, it wouldn't really but it was a good excuse to go a bit mad in the shop!

They loaded the car up.

'Mum, where are we going to put Alan's luggage?' asked Tom as Mum forced the last bag of shopping into the boot.

Mum gasped with horror! 'Crikey!' she exclaimed. 'I hadn't thought about that.' She gazed forlornly at the jam-packed boot. 'We'll just have to hope that Alan's travelling light,' she shrugged.

'We could eat some of the food now, if you liked?' offered Kevin.

'I might hold you to that when we get to the airport,' grinned Mum. 'Come on, let's go.'

9
Alan Arrives

They got a bit lost, as usual, but soon found themselves at the airport. Mum opted for the multi-storey car park, even though it was further away from the terminal than the open-air parking.

'I want to repack the boot,' Mum explained, 'and I don't intend getting soaked while I do it.' It was still raining.

The boys fidgeted and bickered while Mum reorganised the supplies in the boot. She managed to clear a space that, with a bit of luck, Alan's case might fit in to.

'And if it doesn't, I'll fit one of you guys in there instead,' said Mum, 'and shove Alan's stuff on the seat.'

'Bagsy me in the boot!' cried Kevin.

'There'd be no food left when we got home then,' grumbled Tom.

'Come on, just time for a drink before Alan's plane gets in,' said Mum, checking her watch. She was looking forward to seeing Alan. He was a very special person to her. Kevin noticed Mum smiling happily to herself. He nudged Tom. 'Your mum's gone all lovey-dovey, look.'

Tom ignored him. He really liked Alan but he was a bit jealous. For so long it had been just him and Mum and Anna. That was the way he liked it. He continued to sulk until they got into the terminal. It was large and airy and full of shops and cafés. Mum and Anna headed for those. There was also an enormous fishpond with some huge goldfish in it. Kevin stared at them in amazement. Tom joined him reluctantly.

'Look at the size of those things!' marvelled Kevin. 'If you fell in, they'd swallow you whole.'

'Wish Alan would fall in then,' grumbled Tom.

Kevin turned to his friend.

'Just what is it with you about Alan?' he demanded. 'You've been a grotbag ever since we got here just because Alan's coming. He's a nice guy, and he's nuts about your mum and you and Anna. You should be glad he's around.'

'I know, Kev,' sighed Tom, sitting down on the edge of the pond. 'I know. And I like Alan a lot, but, well, what about Dad?'

'He's been dead three years, Tom,' said Kevin gently, sitting beside Tom. 'That's a long time for you guys to be on your own. Your mum must have been really lonely without him. And you don't have to stop loving your dad just because Alan's here now.'

'Yeah, that's what Mum said to me,' admitted Tom. 'She said she still loves Dad too, and always will. But she says there's room in her heart for Alan as well.'

'Yes, I can imagine your mum saying that,' smiled Kevin. 'She says really nice things like that. So don't beat yourself up about it. It'll all work out, you'll see.'

Tom nodded, knowing Kevin was right. 'Come on,' he said, jumping up. 'Race you to the arrivals gate.'

The boys had to weave through the crowds of people, occasionally not weaving quite enough and getting tangled up with suitcases or trolleys. At last they arrived, breathless, at the gate to watch for Alan coming through. Mum and Anna were already there.

'I thought I'd lost you,' Mum frowned, but her frown disappeared almost at once as she caught sight of Alan emerging, thankfully only holding a very small suitcase and a couple of carrier bags full of interesting looking parcels.

Alan spotted them and ran over at once. He kissed Mum and Anna and hugged them all in turn.

'Hi gang!' he grinned. 'Great to see you all again. And I've got a holiday present for each of you too.' Anna danced round in excitement as he delved into the bags and handed out a package to each of them in turn.

'Cool, thanks Alan,' cried Kevin, ripping the wrapping paper off his in delight. Beneath it he found a Jungle Mission car and outfit for his Action Man. 'Mad!' he breathed in wonder. 'We just got some Action Man stuff at the shop. Different stuff though,' he added hastily in case Alan thought he was being ungrateful.

Tom got the same as Kevin. 'So there'll be no fighting,' explained Alan.

'Thanks, Alan,' smiled Tom happily. He was thrilled with the Action Man set. Maybe Alan would be OK as a dad after all!

Anna got a Barbie rucksack and Mum got a bottle of really expensive perfume. She blushed with pleasure. They went back to the car chatting happily, telling Alan about everything they'd seen and done so far. Somehow the bad weather didn't matter so much now that Alan had arrived.

They played card games that night as they listened to the rain falling and the river rushing. Mum peered out into the gloom.

'It's definitely rising,' she said anxiously. 'And that's even with the barrage helping to control the flow.'

Yes, you must take me to see that barrage,' said Alan. 'And that tunnel you found. How about tomorrow?'

It's a deal,' said Kevin. 'And don't worry Mrs D, I bet the rain stops tonight.'

It didn't. It got heavier instead.

10
Still Raining

Tom groaned when he woke up and heard the steady drumming on the canvas.

'This is getting boring,' he muttered crossly as he snuggled back into his sleeping bag.

'What is?' came Alan's voice.

Tom wriggled out of his warm cocoon on the floor of the main room of the tent. Now that Alan was here he and Kevin had moved out of the second sleeping compartment of the tent. Alan had said they could stay but it was a bit of a squash with three of them in there so they'd opted for the living room floor instead.

Alan was making a cup of tea.

'The rain's boring,' yawned Tom. 'It just doesn't stop.'

'Like our teacher!' That was Kevin, sounding a bit muffled from inside his sleeping bag.

'It was lovely and sunny when we first got here,' Tom told Alan. 'But that seems like years ago now. All it does is rain these days.'

'And I didn't come here to be rained on,' smiled Alan. 'I get enough of that when I visit you guys in

Ireland!' Alan lived and worked in England.

'Yeah, well we live in Ireland, don't forget. We get full-time rain and you only get it part-time. We deserve sunshine even more than you do.' Kevin again.

'Maybe it'll clear up later,' said Alan hopefully.

'Maybe.' Tom tried to sound and feel optimistic — but failed.

'Well, you can still take me to this tunnel of yours, can't you?' suggested Alan. 'We can wrap up in our rain jackets.'

Tom sat up and stretched, then shivered in the chilly damp air of the tent. 'It'll be mega mega muddy,' he warned. 'It was boggy enough on a dry day.'

'Well, this campsite is pretty boggy from what I can see,' observed Alan peering out of the plastic window in the side of the tent. He whistled. 'That river looks a bit wild!'

'Does it?' That was Mum, coming out of her sleeping compartment. 'Let me see.' She joined Alan at the window. She gave a cry of alarm. 'We're going to get washed away!'

Alan put his arm round her. 'We're OK. The river's angry but I don't think it's dangerous.'

Mum didn't look convinced. 'I don't feel safe so

close to it, not with all this rain. Honestly, I'd feel happier if we could move to another site, further away from the river. I could go and ask the camp supervisor after breakfast.'

'OK, it's probably as well,' acknowledged Alan. 'The boys have offered to show me their tunnel this morning.'

'And the guard bats!' piped up Kevin.

'Ugh! It'll be muddy,' shuddered Mum.

'That's what we said,' nodded Tom. 'But Alan doesn't mind. And neither do we. Do we Kev? Kev loves mud. He went swimming in it at the tunnel, Alan.'

'He did? Why am I not surprised?' laughed Alan.

A little wail came from the sleeping compartment. Mum went to see Anna. She re-emerged a few moments later, looking worried.

'Poor Anna! She's burning up!' explained Mum. 'Where's the Calpol.' She rummaged in the food-cum-first-aid cupboard. 'I'll have to leave you guys to go exploring in the mud on your own this morning. Anna needs to stay in bed. Mind you, it's probably because of this damp that she's got poorly.' Mum looked grim.

'Maybe we'd better think about moving to a

hotel then,' said Alan, concerned. 'At least, just until the weather clears up.'

'Wow, one with a swimming pool and a telly, like the one we stopped at on our way here?' Tom liked the sound of that.

Mum smiled. 'That was a special treat, love! And hideously expensive. We'll have to go to a less flashy one. There were a couple in the town I noticed.'

'Good. I'll check them out later,' Alan promised.

Mum disappeared back to see Anna. They heard some sobs.

'Poor Annie,' said Kevin. 'Being ill on holiday is the pits.'

'Let's have breakfast,' said Alan. 'What do you lads want?'

'Mum nips off for croissants and stuff from the boulangerie in the village square,' Tom informed him. 'Well, at least she did, until it started raining the other day. We've been having cereal since then.'

'I didn't come to France for cereal,' smiled Alan. 'I'll wrap up and go and find this bakery. I'll follow my nose. I think I'll see if I can get some take-away coffee from somewhere too.' Alan peered mournfully into his lukewarm, weak tea. 'I'd forgotten how awful tea made over a stove is!'

'In that case, bring me a coffee too, please!' Mum called from the sleeping compartment.

'As good as done!' said Alan as he put on his rain jacket. As he unzipped the door of the tent a squall of rain blew in. Some of it landed on Tom and Kevin. They protested loudly.

'Sorry!' called Alan, but not looking it. 'That'll make you get up anyway.'

It did. They were dressed, in damp clothes, by the time Alan got back, loaded down with goodies. He had two boxes of croissants and gateaux for breakfast, two big bars of chocolate, two huge take-away coffees and three bottles of Coca-Cola for the children. Mum looked disapproving when she saw those.

'Coke for breakfast?'

Alan shrugged. 'We all need a boost on a rotten morning like this.'

'True,' sighed Mum. 'I give in.'

They sat down and tucked in. Anna snuggled up on Mum's lap. Even the stickiest cakes and the chocolate couldn't tempt her.

'I'll have her share,' offered Tom greedily.

'No you won't, we'll save it until Anna feels a bit better,' Mum told him. 'Besides, you'll explode if you eat any more.'

'Kevin will blow first,' Tom told her. 'He's way greedier than me. And Alan's on his third cake.'

'Tell-tale,' said Alan indistinctly, through a mouthful of pastry and cream.

Eventually they were all full. Anna had fallen asleep so Mum put her back to bed. Alan and the boys got ready to go exploring. Mum gave Alan the keys to the car so they could drive to the wood where the tunnel was. There was no way they could cycle in this downpour.

'What are you going to do, Mrs D?' asked Kevin.

'Pack,' announced Mum firmly. There was no answer to that.

11
Water, Water Everywhere

It didn't take Mum long to pack. They had travelled light and been living out of their suitcases. Mum cleaned the kitchen area and swept the floor, in between times checking on Anna. Her daughter didn't look well at all.

'I don't know. What's up with you, honey?' She gave Anna a cuddle. 'Goodness!' she exclaimed. Anna was really hot now. 'Drat, I didn't pack a thermometer. Oh Anna, you're not well at all. I'm going to have to find a doctor. I'll have to get Alan back here.'

Mum laid Anna carefully on the bed again and rummaged in her handbag for her mobile phone. She turned it on and punched in the code. The display flashed into life and informed Mum it was 'searching' for a signal, but it didn't find one. Several minutes later it was still 'searching'.

'Anna, I'm just popping outside,' called Mum. 'I can't get a signal for the phone. It might be because of the tent. Let's hope so.'

Mum threw her raincoat over her head and unzipped the door. To stop too much wind and rain getting in, she only unzipped it a little way and tried to squeeze through a small gap. But she caught her foot and tripped, landing with a splash in the big puddle of water outside the doorway. The phone landed in the puddle too, and promptly stopped working. Mum swore. She picked herself up, and then the phone, and crawled back into the tent.

'Stupid fool!' she cursed herself. Now what?

She went back to Anna. Anna looked very feverish.

'I can't risk waiting,' Mum thought out loud. The fear of meningitis was lurking in her mind. 'I must get you to a doctor straight away.'

Wet and muddy as she was, Mum pulled on her raincoat properly. She bundled the droopy Anna into her kagoule and wrapped a blanket round her as well. Then, struggling under the little girl's weight, she set off. The campsite office was firmly closed so Mum decided to head for the tourist office in the town. She hoped and prayed it would be open. It was the tourist season after all, although you wouldn't have thought so. The place was deserted. People were sensibly staying indoors out of the rain.

Just then, a loud rumbling sound broke through the drumming of the rain. Mum stopped and listened.

'Crikey, whatever was that?' she wondered. Anna just grunted. 'It seemed to be coming from upriver.' Mum was still close to the river. She peered through the trees and driving rain but drops of water kept getting in her eyes. 'Maybe it was thunder.' Suddenly an ear-splitting klaxon sounded.

'What the . . .!' Mum jumped in alarm. Anna started to cry. 'Where did that come from?' cried Mum, in panic. Without knowing why, she began to run, or rather stagger along, clutching Anna. Then she stopped, frozen to the spot with fear. Through the rain, she caught sight of a wall of water, a metre or so high, surging towards her, along the river and the banks. She turned and ran for her life away from the river. She hardly noticed Anna's weight now and she certainly didn't feel one of her shoes come off as she tore through some mud.

Mum glanced back to the wall of water. She wasn't out of its path yet, and she wasn't going to get clear in time. She had to get off the ground! But how? There were no climbable trees or cars to crawl on. But there was the climbing frame in the playground, just a bit further on. That would do.

Mum blasted towards it as the water roared towards her. She grasped one of the metal struts and hauled herself and Anna up. She felt an excruciating stab of pain in her back but this wasn't the time to worry about it. One more heave and she and Anna were at the top of the frame. And at that precise moment the wave of water smashed into the frame. Mum felt the metal shake under the impact. She clung on for grim death as the water tore her other shoe off and carried it away with all the other debris it had collected — rubbish, branches, even a cat. Mum shuddered when she saw that. She watched in horror as the water crashed into the tents, including the tent where she and Anna had been until less than five minutes ago. A few people had struggled out when the klaxon sounded. What was happening to them, or to all the poor people still in their tents? There was nothing she could do to help anyway. All that concerned her now was keeping Anna safe.

'Alan, look after the boys!' she begged before fear and shock overtook her and she began to shake uncontrollably. Below her the swollen river rushed catastrophically onwards.

SHANNONBRIDGE LIBRARY

12
Tunnel of Terror

The boys had eventually managed to navigate Alan to the wood by the river where the tunnel was. They'd taken a good few wrong turns on the way.

'Haven't you got a sense of direction?' Alan had asked, exasperated after being told yet again that 'actually, Alan, I don't think this is right'.

'A sense of humour, yes!' Kevin had said.

'And a sense of adventure, definitely,' Tom had added. 'But a sense of direction, I guess not. Sorry Alan.'

But at last they were where they should be. They reluctantly left the warmth and dryness of the car and set off in the driving rain. Kevin pointed out the first path they'd taken before reaching the proper one. It was certainly an awful lot muddier than last time, even before they got to where the drop was. When they got there, Alan peered down at the orange mud.

'Do I really want to jump down into that?' he wondered aloud.

Even Kevin and Tom hesitated.

'Oh, come on. We might as well, now we're here.' Alan eased himself down as gently as he could into the mud. He sunk in to the height of his ankles. The boys watched fascinated as a huge air bubble popped and mud began to slide into his runners.

'Oooh, I can feel it oozing round my toes!' Alan pulled a face. 'Yuck!'

Kevin plopped down next to him. His shoes filled up too. Tom pulled his favourite runners off and hung them round his neck with his socks rolled into them.

'I'd rather go in my bare feet than drag a pile of mud around with me,' he told the others.

'Good idea,' nodded Alan. 'But I'm leaving mine on. I'll only get filthy hands if I take them off now. I think I'll just have to squelch along.'

'Me too,' said Kevin. 'Come on, let's squelch quietly and surprise those bats. Follow me!'

Kevin flicked his torch on and set off. Alan plodded along behind him. Finally Tom followed gingerly. He stubbed his toe a couple of times on rocks on the ground but on the whole he was glad not to be covering his runners in mud. But the three didn't squelch particularly quietly, so they didn't hear the rumbling noise Mum had heard. All they could hear was syrupy slurps of orange mud.

They were nearly up to the bats' roost when the klaxon sounded.

'Holy moly!' exclaimed Kevin. Then, 'Hey, oy, get out of my face!' he spluttered as the bats, startled by the sudden sound, fluttered around in panic.

'Easy! They won't fly into you,' Alan calmed him. 'They can't see you but they can sense where you are with their sonar. But what on earth was that noise? Have you heard that before?'

'No!' Tom looked anxious. 'Maybe we'd better go back. Mum might be worried.'

Alan smiled to himself. As always, Tom was worried about his mother. But then, so was he now.

'Yes, I guess we'd better. We'll come and wade through this mud again another day.'

As they turned round they became aware of a rushing, roaring noise.

'Hey, what's that?' demanded Kevin, in a shrill, scared voice.

'It sounds like . . . Oh help! It's the river! Look!' Tom clutched at Alan and pointed. A wave of muddy water was surging up the tunnel towards them. 'We're trapped!'

'RUN! RUN!' bellowed Alan, dragging Tom in front of him and turning to head along the tunnel.

'It goes uphill. We'll get clear of the water!'

'I hope so!' cried Kevin. Bending low, they charged for all they were worth away from the water. It was worst for Alan. He was quite tall and kept clipping his head on the ceiling. The tunnel floor got rocky under Tom's feet. They hurt like mad but he didn't care. Water was round his ankles. Something bumped him. He looked down and saw it was one of Alan's shoes!

'Come on, lads. Keep going!' shouted Alan. Kevin lunged forward but caught his elbow on the tunnel wall. The torch flew from his hand.

'I'm sorry! I'm sorry!' he babbled. There was confusion for a moment. Alan bumped into Kevin hard, and they both fell with a splash into the water that was up to their knees now. The tunnel entrance they had come through was totally submerged. Tom skidded to a halt and stood, totally disorientated in the darkness. But it wasn't quite pitch black. His eyes quickly adjusted to the dark and he saw the familiar hint of daylight ahead.

'Not far to go,' he shouted, groping for Alan in the gloom. Alan was standing up. He straightened up too much and whacked his head on the tunnel ceiling again. 'Ow!' he cursed angrily. 'Kevin, are you OK?' He heaved the boy up out of the water.

'Yeah!' gasped Kevin.

'Good, now come on, hurry!'

Alan pushed Tom in front of him. They couldn't go as quickly now. Although they could see daylight ahead, not much light was filtering into the tunnel. But the water lapping round their legs was a good incentive to keep going. At last they cleared the water as the tunnel sloped upwards and soon, thank goodness, they were standing in the secret chamber.

'Better climb out of this hollow, and fast,' Alan said.

'So no chance of a quick rest then?' panted Kevin.

'No way!' exclaimed Tom. 'We've got to go back and get Mum.'

'Oh no! I'd forgotten all about Mrs D and Annie!' cried Kevin. 'What are we waiting for?'

They clambered up the steep sides of the gully. Alan didn't even notice the interesting rock formations they passed. As a speleologist, or cave scientist, normally such things would fascinate him and demand his attention for hours on end. But not today. There were far more urgent matters to worry about.

Within minutes they had reached the top. They turned towards the wood and the river.

'My word!' Alan shook his head at the sight. There was water everywhere. The woods below them were flooded. Beyond them, the river churned.

'The world's turned into a river!' gasped Kevin.

'Oh no!' cried Tom. 'Look! There are tents in the river, and all sorts of stuff! We've got to get Mum!' He began to run towards the woods.

'Hey!' Alan called.

Tom ignored him and kept running.

'You're going the wrong way!' Alan called. 'We need to circle behind the woods to get back to the car — if we can. Come on.'

Tom felt a bit stupid as he sprinted back to the others. But Alan smiled. 'You're a brave lad, Tom. We'll get your mum and Anna, don't worry.' He sounded confident but he didn't feel it. Not one little bit.

13
Panic All Round

Mum continued to cling on desperately to the climbing frame. But she'd noticed that either the water was rising or else the climbing frame was sinking. She rather thought it was the latter. She'd been watching the water and gauging its height against a fir tree close by. It was just below a branch and that hadn't changed since the wall of water had first swamped the land. But now her legs were in the water up to her knees. Mum guessed, correctly as it happened, that the water was making the ground beneath the climbing frame waterlogged and soft. The frame was sinking slowly and Mum didn't dare move for fear of making things worse.

'Mummy, why are we in the river?' asked Anna suddenly. She'd been pretty dazed for a while but now she was aware of what was going on.

'Well, sweetie, the river burst its banks and we were in the way so it caught us, I'm afraid,' she explained. 'But don't worry, we're safe here. Mummy's got you. Someone will come and rescue us soon.'

'Alan and the boys?' asked Anna.

Mum faked a smile. 'Yes, they'll be here.' She was worried sick about them. What if the flood had caught them too? What if they'd been trapped in that tunnel? She could hardly bear to think about that. What she did think about, though, was what had caused the flood. It was too sudden to have been caused just by the rainfall. A whole lot of extra water had come from somewhere. Had those ecowarrior people blown up the dam after all like Kevin suggested? Perhaps that klaxon had been a warning as the dam gave way.

Help was very slow arriving, Mum thought. She felt like they'd been there for hours, but actually it was only a few minutes. A few figures were gathering at the edge of the water on higher ground, looking hopelessly on at the scene. Mum noticed there were a few other stranded people, desperately hanging onto trees that now stuck out of the deep water.

'Au secours! Please get us off!' begged Mum.

Meanwhile the boys and Alan had got back to the car. It was up to the top of its wheels in water. The water was flowing fast, but not too fast, so they were able to wade safely to it. Alan unlocked the front door. There was water on the floor to a depth of fifteen centimetres or so. They sloshed inside.

Alan turned the ignition key and the car made a wheezing sound. The next time Alan tried it didn't make any sound at all. Alan thumped the steering wheel in frustration.

'If only I had one of my jeeps,' moaned Alan. When Alan went on field trips to study caves, he took one of the university's robust landrovers.

'Well you don't, you've got our crappy car,' snapped Tom, in a sudden fury. Moaning wasn't going to save Mum and Anna.

Alan nodded. 'Sorry,' he said quietly. Tom was right. It was no good wishing for things he hadn't got. He had to make do with what was on hand.

'The car needs lots of choke when it rains,' Tom told him.

'OK.' Alan pulled the manual choke out as far as it would go.

'And lots of revs when you start her up,' went on Tom. 'She's very sensitive to the weather, Mum says.'

Alan did as he'd been advised. This time when he turned the key, the engine reluctantly coughed into life.

'Thanks, Tom,' said Alan apologetically.

'Bingo!' whooped Kevin. 'Let's go get the girls!'

They could only drive very slowly through the water. Several times the wheels started spinning and the engine almost stalled. But Alan nursed the car out of the flood water and back onto dry land. They weren't on a road any more — that had disappeared. Alan had to drive through fields, and hedges.

'I'm not normally an environmental lout like this,' he explained to the boys as they barged their way through a line of bushes that separated two fields. The branches scratched angrily at the side of the car and the passenger side wing mirror came off.

'I'll get the car repaired when we get home,' promised Alan.

'Talking about environmental louts,' Kevin piped up, 'd'you think those ecowarriors are to blame for this, Tom? I reckon they blew up the barrage, don't you?'

'Ecowarriors?' echoed Alan, avoiding some startled sheep. 'What do you mean?'

Kevin told Alan what they'd seen at the barrage, pausing now and again to hang grimly onto his seat as the going got rough.

'They were protesting about the dam, but surely they wouldn't risk destroying loads of countryside by blowing it up to make the river flood, would they?' asked Tom.

Alan shrugged. 'It seems unlikely, it's true. But possible. Or maybe something else happened to destroy the barrage, or maybe it's still intact but just couldn't hold any more water back?'

'I'm sure we'll find out soon enough, but it's a puzzle,' frowned Tom.

Just then Alan came to a road again.

'It's leading the right way, thank goodness.' He accelerated at once. The road deposited them onto the main road into St Jean les Bains. It was just clear of the flood. They all gasped to see the amount of traffic heading out of the town. Cars were bumper to bumper as people attempted to flee the danger.

'Crikey, they're expecting more trouble by the look of it,' observed Kevin.

'Probably just panicking,' said Alan.

'Well, they should be trying to help people who got caught in the flood, like Mum!' Tom's voice gave way as the tears started.

'People like that wouldn't be any help anyway,' Alan told him. 'The gendarmes will have everything under control, I bet. Streuth!'

The cry came as Alan rounded a bend to find a truck driving towards him on the wrong side of the road. Alan swerved off into a ditch, throwing them about a lot. The truck thundered by without stopping, followed by a stream of cars, all on the wrong side of the road too.

'Everyone OK?' Alan asked shakily when they had crunched to a stop.

'What's that you said about the police controlling stuff?' asked Kevin, rubbing his nose which he'd bashed on Alan's seat, despite being strapped in. 'You OK, Tom?'

'Yeah . . . just mad.'

'Looks like I'm wrong about the police. Blast it!' Alan thumped the dashboard. 'Come on, we'll have to continue on foot. This car is wrecked, thanks to those fools.'

'Poor old car,' said Kevin, sliding out of the back door. Tom and Alan had to climb out of that door too since they couldn't open theirs. The car was pretty messed up at the front.

They jogged along the side of the road as quickly as their wobbly legs would carry them. They'd all had quite a shock from the crash. They got to the outskirts of town and ran with renewed energy towards the campsite. Or rather, towards where the campsite had been. It was just water now. Only the campsite manager's office remained visible, its top third sticking up above the raging torrent.

They stood at the edge of the water in what used to be the town square, next to the tennis courts, and stared in horror.

'Mum! Mum!' yelled Tom. 'Where are you?' He started to wade out into the water but Alan grabbed him and yanked him back.

'Tom, get real!' he snapped. 'You'd be washed away by that. Where on earth are some properly equipped rescuers?'

Just as he spoke, they heard the clatter of a helicopter.

'At last,' sighed Kevin. 'But I'm guessing they're a bit late.'

'Don't say that! Don't you dare say that!' fumed Tom, rounding on Kevin. 'Mum's OK. She's safe somewhere, she's got to be! She's got to!'

Alan put an arm round Tom, but Tom shook it angrily off.

'It's all your fault,' he screamed, totally unfairly. 'If you hadn't come, then Mum wouldn't have been left on her own. She'd have taken us shopping or something, or she'd have had the car so she could have got to safety! I hate you!' He began to pummel Alan with his fists. Alan didn't try to stop him. His face was total misery.

'Tom, stop it,' cried Kevin, grabbing his friend's

arms. 'Get a grip! You're being a moron. It's not helping anything.'

Tom shoved Kevin angrily. As he stumbled, Kevin caught sight of the climbing frame sticking out of the water further upstream from the campsite. There was someone on it, no two people surely. An adult and a kid. Kevin strained his eyes trying to get them into focus.

'Look!' he shouted. 'It's them! It's Mrs D and Annie. On the climbing frame, over there. It really is! Mrs D is such a hero!'

'What? Where?' cried Alan. 'Oh yes, I see them. It is them. Oh thank God.'

Tom didn't say anything. He just stared.

'Come on, let's get closer.'

They began to run along the water's edge until they were opposite Mum and Anna.

'We're here! We'll get you!' yelled Tom, jumping up and down.

But Mum didn't hear him. And she didn't look up. She was concentrating on hanging on. Her arms were aching. She was freezing cold and her back was agony. And all the time the climbing frame was subsiding. What was she going to do?

14
Net Gain

'Where's that helicopter gone?' demanded Kevin. 'It should be rescuing Mrs D!'

'It's headed upriver a little way, I think,' said Alan. 'I guess it's sussing out where people are and who's in most danger. Then it'll start rescuing people.'

'Mum's in danger!' cried Tom. 'I'm sure that climbing frame she's on is moving.'

'Is it?' gasped Alan. He stared hard across the foaming water. 'Oh no! I think you're right. The water must be undermining it. If it gives way, they are in serious trouble!'

'Is there anything we can do?' asked Kevin. 'There has to be something.'

'If I could get some rope, I could tie it to one of these lampposts and try and swim out to them,' Alan suggested desperately.

'That's too dangerous for two reasons,' said Tom bluntly. 'Firstly you're a pretty hopeless swimmer, and secondly the river is going far too fast.'

'Right both times,' shrugged Alan. 'But we've

got to do something. The official rescuers aren't doing much. Oh, here come some reinforcements.' Two vans of gendarmes pulled up. They bustled around looking important.

'What's that yellow thing coming down the river?' asked Kevin, suddenly. The others looked to where he was pointing.

'It's an upturned canoe, I think,' said Alan.

'And it's heading straight for Mum!' cried Tom. 'Mum, look out, look OUT!' Tom screamed with all his might. This time Mum heard him. She looked first at Tom, her heart jumping with joy at the sight of seeing the three of them safe and sound. Then she turned her head to see what Tom was shouting about. An upside-down canoe was hurtling towards her.

Oh no, thought Mum. If that thing hits the frame, it'll knock us over for sure. But if I can grab hold of it, we might be OK.

Mum could just see the piece of the rope at the bow end that was used for dragging the canoe clear of water. She didn't have long to plan what to do, just a few seconds. Heaving Anna up as high as she could with one arm, which was hooked through the frame, she stretched out with the other. The frame groaned and moved with her movement. She heard

Tom's cry of alarm from the bank. But in the next instant, the canoe slammed into the frame. Mum grabbed the rope and tugged it upwards with strength she didn't know she had. She twisted it as she did so and the canoe turned the right way up.

The climbing frame began to fall over into the water, but as it did so, Mum jumped onto the canoe. She balanced on it for just a second or so, but it was long enough for her to bundle Anna into the front cockpit. She had hoped she might be able to make a lunge for the back cockpit but the canoe bounced off the climbing frame and shook her off balance. She slid into the water.

'Mummy!' shrieked Anna. But Mum had a firm hold of the rope still and she had her other arm over the nose of the canoe. As she clung onto it, the current swept the canoe downstream.

'Mummy!' screamed Anna again.

'It's OK!' yelled Mum, above the roar of the river. 'Just sit very still and we'll be fine. Mummy's hanging on tight, don't worry!'

Who am I trying to kid, thought Mum, suddenly remembering all the rocks in the river further down. Her legs would be coming into contact with them in a while unless she could somehow get herself and Anna to shore.

'Now what?' cried Kevin. 'Mrs D's being carried off! Now that's not tennis!'

Kevin had picked up that expression from the TV. Tom had looked at him puzzled the first time Kevin had said it to him.

'You what?' he'd demanded.

'That's not tennis,' Kevin had repeated patiently. 'It means, 'that's not fair'. It comes from this really good programme. There's this old, stuck up English guy and he says it all the time and . . .'

Tom had cut him short at that point with an annoyed look. But now he looked at Kevin with new eyes.

'Tennis! Tennis, of course! Kev, you're brilliant!'

'Well, I know but . . .'

'Come on, both of you. We've got to get the tennis net out of that tennis court NOW!' He pointed to the tennis courts next to them. 'Have you got your penknife, Kev?'

'You betya!' grinned Kevin.

'And I've got one too,' shouted Alan, already sprinting off. 'What's the plan, Tom?'

'Well,' panted Tom, keeping pace with Alan, 'there's this fairly low bridge a couple of kilometres downstream. We saw it when we went canoeing the first day we were here. If we can get there before Mum and lower the net over, we'll catch her.'

'We need to act fast then,' said Alan. 'That river is going fast.'

They were on the court now. Alan dashed to one of the nets and began sawing through it. Kevin attacked the other end with gusto. It wasn't often he got the chance for some serious destruction like this!

'Can we outrun the river?' asked Tom, jiggling up and down beside Alan with impatience.

'We'll try,' said Alan grimly.

Tom hurried over to Kevin.

'Hurry up old buddy!' he begged.

'Boy, this net is tough stuff,' gasped Kevin. 'Or maybe my knife is blunt. Hang on, nearly there. Done!'

Tom grabbed that end of the net and ran back to Alan, who had cut through his side too.

'Gently does it,' cautioned Alan, taking the net carefully out of Tom's hands. 'We don't want to tangle the net now, do we.' Alan folded it neatly, but quickly. He tucked the bundle under his arm and they headed back to the gate. But just then, a fat, elderly man pulled up on a moped. He leapt off angrily, leaving the engine ticking over.

'Looks like trouble!' muttered Kevin. 'I guess he's the tennis court caretaker.'

'Que faites-vous?' the caretaker demanded angrily, confronting them, glaring at the tennis net in Alan's arms.

'Er, er, pour, er save people, pour sauver les gens dans l'eau!' Alan explained.

'Vous ne pouvez pas prendre mon filet!' said the caretaker.

Alan gave up on French. 'Oh grow up, you fool,' he spat. 'People are drowning and all you care about is your stupid net.'

The man lunged at the net in Alan's arms. Alan side-stepped neatly. The man fell flat on his face then began groaning, blood streaming out of his nose.

'I never touched him, now did I?' winked Alan. 'Now, come on, kids, run.'

They got to the gate.

'Look, his moped! Let's nick it!' said Kevin in delight. 'Fat pain-in-the-neck guy doesn't need it at the moment.'

'Good idea, Kevin, but I prefer to use the term "borrow",' said Alan. 'We need wheels if we've any chance of saving the girls. We'll make things up with fatso later. But the moped won't take all three of us. Tom, you come with me. Kevin, can you follow on foot?'

Kevin nodded. He was disappointed at being left behind but he knew there was no choice.

'I'll be fine. Just go.'

Alan jumped on the small machine. Tom squeezed on behind and Alan passed him the net.

'Now how does this thing work?' wondered Alan. 'I guess this is the throttle.' He squeezed the twist grip on the handlebar. The moped leapt forward. Tom grabbed at Alan and just about managed not to fall off.

'We have lift off!' bellowed Alan and they careered off.

Kevin watched them disappear down the road, weaving in and out of the slow moving cars. Then he looked back at the tennis court. The caretaker was sitting up, looking dazed.

'Time to scarper!' grinned Kevin. He set off jogging, but then noticed a bicycle leaning up against a wall. He stopped and battled with his conscience. Should I take it and have a chance to catch up with Alan and Tom and help them save Annie and Mum? Or should I be honest and just carry on jogging? His conscience lost the battle. This was an emergency after all. He'd bring the bike back to this exact spot when everything was over. To be certain of that, he scratched an 'X' on the wall with his penknife, then jumped on and pedalled awkwardly off. The bike was way too big but once he got used to it, he quickly picked up speed. He hurtled off, hot on Tom's trail.

15
Big Fish

'There it is!' cried Tom. 'There's the bridge.' They had just turned a bend in the road and could now see a small track leading down to it.

'Did you see your mum on the way?' called Alan over his shoulder.

'No, but we weren't very close to the river at times,' said Tom. 'We were definitely going faster than the water though. We must have beaten her.' He couldn't bear to think of what might happen if Mum had got ahead of them.

They bounced over the rough track towards the bridge. The water level had risen tremendously. The bridge cleared the river by less than a metre here but at least the flooding hadn't spread far. There were only a few centimetres of water over the land.

Alan drove onto the bridge. He and Tom climbed off the moped. Alan tried to put the bike stand down but it had jammed.

'No time to waste,' he said, dropping the machine down with a crunch. 'Tom, take this end of the net and stay at this side of the bridge. I'll go to the other side.'

Alan jogged away, unravelling the net as he went. It was a good bit shorter than the bridge, Tom noticed. Would they still be able to trap Mum and Anna in it? He felt sick with worry.

'Lean over the parapet a bit more,' Alan called to him.

Tom did. He held the net down beneath him. It just touched the surface of the water.

By leaning a long way over, Alan got his end of the net touching the water too. 'Bingo!' he called, giving Tom a thumbs-up sign.

Tom managed a weak smile back. Now they just had to wait for Mum. Tom looked up the river. Was that her? He thought he saw a yellowy blob heading towards them. Then, horror of horrors, he also saw what looked like a body some distance from the canoe.

'Alan! Mum's fallen off the canoe!' he shouted. Alan peered ahead.

'No, I can see someone holding onto the canoe. That body must be someone else. We'll see if we can get him too. But first let's concentrate on getting the girls. Hold on for all you're worth, Tom, but keep your balance. If you start to feel yourself falling, for goodness sake let go of the net.' Tom nodded.

The canoe with its cargo was bouncing quickly towards them over the choppy water. Clinging desperately to the canoe, Mum's arms ached so much she didn't notice the pain in her back or the freezing cold of the water. Anna huddled shivering and crying quietly in the canoe.

'Good girl,' called Mum, for the hundredth time. 'So far, so good!' What else could she say?

Then she saw the bridge ahead. There wasn't going to be much clearance. In fact, there seemed to be something filling the space above the water. Was that something hanging from the bridge or were her tired eyes deceiving her? She blinked hard. No, they weren't. There were two people on the bridge, a man and a boy. It couldn't be Alan and Tom, could it? Surely they were back in town?

'I'm hallucinating,' Mum muttered.

But as they got closer, Mum saw that it was them, and she saw they were holding a net down over the water.

'Anna, Anna, we're saved!' Mum shouted. 'Alan and Tom are going to catch us in a giant fishing net!'

Mum kicked her legs for all she was worth to try and turn the canoe sideways. She reckoned that they had a better chance of being caught that way. If the canoe hit the net nose on, it might just blast right through it.

'Anna, love, can you get ready to grab hold of the net? I'll grab hold of you from behind so you won't fall.' Mum braced herself against the side of the canoe.

On the bridge, as the canoe bore down on them, Alan suddenly felt worried. What if the plan didn't work? What if the net broke or something? What if he and Tom couldn't drag them out of the water? So Kevin's arrival at that precise moment couldn't have come at a better time. Kevin threw down the borrowed bike, leant over the parapet and grabbed the net in the middle.

'Good man!' said Alan. 'Now, hang on both of you for all your worth. They're here!'

The canoe smacked into the net, almost dragging it out of Tom and Kevin's hands. But they held on, even though the rope cut into their skin. Anna grasped the rope, but only weakly. Her fingers were slipping but then Mum grabbed her from behind, and heaved her upwards.

'Get her, Kev!' cried Mum. Kevin seized the girl's tiny wrists.

'I've got you, Annie!' he shouted and pulled for all he was worth. He landed Anna on the bridge almost as though she were a fish.

Letting go of his part of the net meant, of course, that it sagged. And that was the part Mum was clinging onto so she was submerged for a moment. She kicked back up to the surface, trying to shove the canoe out of the way.

'Hang on, Jane!' shouted Alan. 'Tom, let go of your end now and come and help me this end. You too, Kev. We'll drag the net up with Jane on it from my end.' Alan realised Tom was struggling on his own.

Tom reluctantly did as he was told. His end of the net immediately disappeared under the bridge, taking Mum and the canoe with it. Kevin put his coat over Anna and raced to help Alan while Tom did the same, hoping that Alan's plan would work.

'Come on, heave!' yelled Alan. They heaved on the net, pulling it up, hand over hand. Mum's head reappeared under the bridge. Then, from nowhere, another pair of hands grabbed onto the net. The sudden increase in weight ripped it out of Kevin's hands. Tom held on for a fraction of a second longer, then he lost his grip too. Alan braced himself desperately against the side of the bridge. Tom saw blood pouring from one of Alan's hands as the skin was ripped off. It must have been agonisingly painful but Alan didn't let go. Kevin and Tom lunged for the net again and helped Alan steady it. They began to pull it in again, a much slower, heavier job.

'Where . . . did . . . that . . . guy . . . come . . . from?' panted Kevin.

'Dunno . . . but if we lose Mum . . . 'cos of him . . . I'll kill him,' replied Tom, gasping for breath from all the effort he was expending.

'Not if I get him first,' said Alan grimly. 'I just hope we can rescue them both. Thank goodness this net is tough.'

Alan shouldn't have said that. No sooner were the words out of his mouth than there was a ripping noise. The net began to tear in the middle. Tom gasped in horror.

'Keep pulling!' cried Alan desperately.

Mum and the stranger came into sight again under the bridge.

'It's one of those ecoterrorists, look!' shrieked Kevin. 'I'd recognise that great red beard anywhere. Him and his friends caused this flood. Oy, let go you ratbag.'

Kevin shook the net angrily.

'Hey, stay cool. We might shake Mum off,' Tom told him.

'One more heave, and I can get your Mum I think,' panted Alan. 'You lads keep hold of the net if you possibly can. I'll get Redbeard next, if he's still there.'

'OK,' said Tom. Kevin said nothing. He would have preferred to let Redbeard float away. He didn't deserve to be saved.

They gave a last, huge heave, then Alan let go of the net and reached down for Mum. But Redbeard grabbed his arm! Alan was pulled off balance and slipped but managed to cling onto the parapet with his other arm just as he was about to go over the edge. Tom and Kevin stared in horror.

'Pull your mother in, Tom. NOW!' Alan shouted.

'Come on Kev, we can do it!' cried Tom

'You betya!'

With their last energy they heaved on the net. Mum kicked madly with her legs then stretched one arm up. Her fingers grasped over the top of the parapet.

'Pull, Tom, PULL!' yelled Kevin. He braced one leg against the parapet, then raised the other next to it and heaved with his whole weight. He was leaning backwards. Mum's other hand made it over the parapet. She let go of the net. As she did so, Kevin crashed to the ground, hitting his head hard. Tom dropped the net and grabbed Mum's arm. But he couldn't pull her up. He needed Alan to do that, but Alan was still wrestling with Redbeard. Alan couldn't pull Redbeard up because of the way Redbeard had pulled him over the edge of the bridge. And Redbeard wouldn't let go. The two men were stuck.

'Alan! Help!' cried Tom in alarm.

Alan looked over at Tom. He saw him desperately hanging onto Mum who was desperately hanging onto the bridge. As Alan looked, Mum slipped back a bit. That did it. Taking a mighty risk, Alan let go of the bridge with his free arm and thumped Redbeard on the side of his face. Redbeard loosened his grip fractionally and Alan tore himself free. Redbeard fell back into the water with a splash. He grabbed at the net again. Up on the bridge, Kevin sat up, a bit dazed. The net suddenly slid over his legs. Thinking Mum was still on the other end of it, Kevin grabbed it again.

Meanwhile Alan had dashed to help Tom. He slid his hands under Mum's armpits and pulled her up, out of the water at last. Mum sank into his arms.

'Hey, don't tell me I'm saving Redbeard here,' panted Kevin, still hanging onto the heavy net, his feet braced once more against the parapet. 'I'm letting go, then.'

'No, don't. Come on, we'll get him out, if we can,' said Alan, reluctantly letting go of Mum and helping her sit down. 'He's a human being after all. Tom, can you help too?'

Between them, it didn't take long to get Redbeard out. He slumped into a heap on the parapet. They left him there and turned to Mum and Anna. Mum had dragged herself over to Anna and was fussing over her.

'Alan, can you get her to a doctor quickly, please,' she whispered.

'I need to get you both to a doctor. Jane, you were amazing. You're one brave woman,' Alan said, hugging both her and Anna.

'No, you're the brave ones,' smiled Mum. 'Really brave . . .' Mum didn't say any more because she suddenly fainted.

'Mum!' cried Tom.

'It's OK,' soothed Alan, as he held Tom's mother in his arms. 'Your mum will be fine. She's exhausted, that's all. Kevin, can you lift Anna up? I reckon I can just about get the three of us on the moped and go and get help.'

'Sure,' said Kevin. 'Come on Annie.'

'I want you boys to stay here, OK? And if Redbeard gives you any trouble, throw him back into the river, right?' Alan grinned.

'Maybe we'll just throw him in anyway,' said Kevin grimly.

Mum came to a few moments later. She was weak and groggy but managed to hang onto Alan on the moped. Anna sat on Alan's lap. The boys watched as the moped limped off, then went to stand guard over Redbeard who was whimpering quietly.

'Not a bad day's work,' said Kevin. 'Even if I say so myself. Eh, Tom? Help!' Kevin suddenly found himself enveloped in a huge hug from Tom.

'We saved them, Kev. We did it! Thanks, buddy!'

Kevin hugged his friend back, very, very tightly.

16
News for Mum

'Hiya Mum!' cried Tom, loaded down with grapes and chocolates. He dumped them unceremoniously onto the bedside cabinet and gave Mum a big kiss and a gentle hug. Mum had a couple of broken ribs, which she'd got either from being bumped against the canoe in the water or when she was being dragged out of the river. She also had a very stiff back. Hospital was the best place for her.

Alan and Kevin followed Tom into Mum's private room.

'We've just been to see Anna in the children's ward, and she's heaps better,' Tom went on.

'I know, I got the nurse to wheel me up there earlier. I was with her most of the morning until my back got too sore sitting up,' Mum told him.

'Well, the three of us will take turns to visit her this afternoon. I just saw the doctor and he said she'll be discharged tomorrow,' said Alan, sitting on the bed beside Mum and squeezing her hand. 'Sorry we couldn't get here sooner. There was a bit of sorting out to do this morning — you know, insurance and stuff.'

Mum groaned. 'Poor you. What a nightmare! The tent, all our stuff, the car and medical bills and somewhere to stay till we can get home and . . .' Mum suddenly looked overwhelmed.

'It's OK, love,' Alan told her, smiling. 'Everything's being taken care of. Thank goodness you took out that travel insurance — it covers everything. It just took a couple of phone calls. The car's been towed off to a garage and the damage isn't too bad apparently. It'll be ready in a few days. The lads and I went shopping for clothes this morning, as you can see.' Tom and Kevin did twirls for Mum so she could see their new French outfits. Mum giggled. 'And as for where we're staying, well . . .'

'Oh, let me tell Mrs D, please!' begged Kevin.

'Go on!' laughed Alan.

'We're in a five star hotel!' boasted Kevin.

'Crikey, are you sure the insurance will cover that?' gasped Mum.

'It doesn't have to,' grinned Kevin, 'that's the great part. You know Redbeard?'

Mum looked puzzled.

'Oh, I guess you didn't get to see him really. He was that guy who suddenly grabbed the net when we were trying to rescue you and he nearly pulled Alan into the water. Anyway, Alan thumped him one but then we pulled him out of the water too. Well, actually it was me who stopped him drowning in the first place.' Kevin tried to look modest.

'Rubbish! You wanted to chuck him back in the river!' Tom reminded him. 'I stopped you.'

'I s'pose,' shrugged Kevin. 'But anyway, it turns out he's the mayor's son. And when the mayor found out we'd rescued him, he said he could never repay us, even though his son is an ecoterrorist. He put us up in this posh hotel.'

Mum still looked pretty puzzled.

'That's the short version of what happened,' smiled Alan. 'After I left the boys to get you and Anna to the hospital on that moped, the gendarmes in the helicopter reappeared and radioed for a land-based rescue crew to pick up the boys and our friend Redbeard. He was in a pretty bad way, but Tom and Kev had put coats on him to keep him warm and the rescuers said that helped save him. These gendarmes recognised who he was and . . .'

' . . . next thing,' butted in Tom, 'the mayor rolled up in a flashy car and went off in the ambulance to hospital with us and Redbeard. That's where we met up with Alan again. Then the mayor found us and took us to the hotel!'

'Goodness,' said Mum weakly, her head reeling.

'But then we went out again because Alan wanted to find the tennis court guy.'

'Who?' asked Mum.

'The guy whose moped we borrowed,' Kevin told her. 'And his tennis net. He was a pain. He tried to stop us taking the net to save you. But then Alan thumped him—'

'No I didn't!' protested Alan.

'Well, you wanted to,' said Kevin, 'and you would have if he hadn't fallen over and knocked himself out.'

'Wow, you've done a fair bit of thumping,' observed Mum, raising an eyebrow at Alan.

'Only one thump,' Alan corrected her. 'And I had to.'

'That's OK then,' smiled Mum. 'And did you find this tennis court guy?'

'Eventually, in a bar. He was a bit unfriendly to start with, wasn't he Alan?'

'Yep, I learnt some new French swear words,' nodded Alan. 'But I promised to pay for a new net and also for borrowing his moped so he was OK.'

'Oh dear, how much will you have to pay?' asked Mum.

'Nothing!' grinned Tom. 'Turns out the mayor's brother runs that bar. When he heard what was going on, he phoned his brother. The mayor turned up and there was lots of shouting then hugging and apparently the town council will pay for the net and the moped. Fair enough, if you ask me.'

'Sounds fair to me too!' agreed Mum.

'Anyway, there's going to be loads of money from the government to clear up the mess. Honestly, Mum you should see it. The town's a disaster zone!'

'But what caused the flood?' asked Mum. 'Was it the ecoterrorists blowing up the barrage? I heard a loud rumbling noise before the wave of water hit us. It sounded like an explosion.'

'That was a landslide!' burst out Tom. 'Well, a rockslide. You remember the quarry we saw with the huge heap of stones by the river? The rain made the heap unstable and it slid into the river. That caused something like a tidal wave that went roaring down the river . . .'

'. . . and it went right over the barrage and broke one of the gates so all the water trapped behind it came rushing out too!' Kevin finished triumphantly. Tom glared at him.

'I was telling Mum!' he pouted.

'Sorry,' said Kevin, not looking very apologetic. 'And when the dam broke a hooter thing went off. We heard that, did you?'

Mum nodded. 'I certainly did. Then all I heard after that was water . . .'

She trailed off, suddenly feeling tearful. She still wasn't quite over the shock of what had happened to them all. Alan saw her expression.

'Hey you boys! Why don't you go and see Anna? If you find that nice nurse in the pink uniform, you know the one who speaks English, why don't you ask if you can take Anna for a ride in a wheelchair? You could bring her here.'

'You bet!' cried Kevin, leaping up. 'Bagsy I push!'

'You? No way! You're a rotten pusher!' protested Tom. They hurtled off.

'Got you to myself for a few minutes,' grinned Alan, giving Mum a kiss. 'You know, I really shouldn't let you guys out of my sight. You manage to get into all kinds of trouble without me. I mean first volcanoes, then avalanches, and now a flood. I'm going to have to do something about it.'

'Oh?' smiled Mum. 'And what might that be?'

'I need you to answer a question for me.'

Mum shrugged. 'OK, fire away,' she said, intrigued.

Alan cleared his throat.

'Jane, will you marry me . . .'